Hello students,

I am giving this book to you to take home because reading is fun and helps you learn. I hope you will read it many times and enjoy it as I have. Thank you for working so hard in school.

Your friend,

Janet Napolitano

Governor Janet Napolitano

Special Thanks to Sponsors

Don't Call Me Pig!
A JAVELINA STORY

WRITTEN BY

Conrad J. Storad

ILLUSTRATED BY

Beth Neely and Don Rantz

The RGU Group

Being Different Makes All The Difference™

Tempe, Arizona

The illustrations were rendered in watercolor and with pen and ink
The text type was set in Esprit Medium
The display type was set in Latiara
Composed in the United States of America
Art direction and design by Trina Stahl
Editing by Conrad J. Storad
Production supervision by Todd Atkins

Printed in China

First impression

Library of Congress Catalog Card Number: 98–65001—Softcover

International Standard Book Number: 1-891795-01-5—Softcover

The RGU Group

www.theRGUgroup.com

33 32 31 30 29 28 27 26 25 24 23 (sc)

For Katelyn and Austin James, my newest niece and nephew.
Never stop reading. Never stop learning!

—CONRAD J. STORAD

For Adam and Amy, our nephew and niece; and Hana Horne, Hannah,
and Sparki at the Heritage Park Zoo in Prescott, Arizona.

—BETH NEELY & DON RANTZ

Welcome to my story
Please pay attention well
I'm an odd-looking creature
And I have a tale to tell.

I am a Javelina (*Hah vuh LEENA*)
But I have other names, you see
In hot, dry Arizona
I'm called Collared Peccary.

My body is thin and muscular
Among cactus and pines I roam
I like the rocky scrubland
The Sonoran Desert is my home.

I live with lots of family members
The herd can grow quite big
Though I'm shy, I've one request
Don't ever call me pig!

I am a Javelina
Look close, I have no tail
I live in Southwestern deserts
With coyotes, jackrabbits, and quail.

My fur is coarse and bristly,
Black and gray with a collar of white
My dark eyes are small and beady
It's true, I have bad eyesight.

My snout is tough as leather
Both plants and fruit I eat
I like the taste of bugs and snakes
Prickly Pear cactus is a treat.

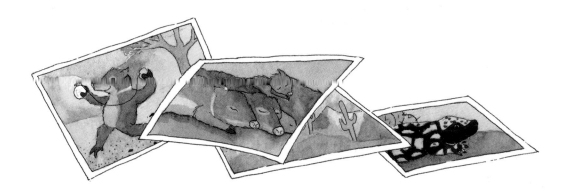

My front teeth are shaped like javelins
The Spaniards thought it so
I use my snout and teeth for digging
Gobble roots and berries where they grow.

When danger's near, I stand my ground
My safety does not matter
A loud grunt signals to my herd
"In all directions . . . SCATTER!"

My skinny legs have just three toes
It's my head that grows quite big
But if you want to keep me happy
Don't ever call me pig!

I am a Javelina,
Not a pig at all, you see
In the wilds of the Southwestern deserts
I'm called Collared Peccary.

My scent is strong and stinky
Sniff . . . you might smell me near
Look close, you may never see me
Only grunting sounds you'll hear.

I have scent glands below each eye
A big one along my back
I use the smell to mark herd land
To know members of my pack.

I weigh as much as sixty pounds
Stand two feet tall, that's big
Just one thing you should remember
Don't ever call me pig!

I am a Javelina
Not a pig at all, you see
In Arizona, New Mexico, and Texas
I'm called Collared Peccary.

Now you know my story
One last thing before I run
Tell your friends about Javelina
Because learning is always fun.

Javelina or Collared Peccary *[Tayassu tajacu]*

Weight:	35 to 60 pounds
Height:	18 to 24 inches at the shoulder
Length:	34 to 40 inches, tip of snout to rump
Diet:	Roots, fruit, cacti, and seeds. Prickly pear cactus is a favorite treat. Will eat snakes, lizards, insects, and grubs
Color:	Grizzled gray or black with yellow tinge on cheeks. White collar runs from shoulder to shoulder
Range:	Deserts, pine forests, and grasslands of Arizona, New Mexico, and southwestern Texas south through Mexico and Central America to the jungles and grasslands of Brazil and Argentina

THE COLLARED PECCARY is a piglike animal, but not actually a pig. The name refers to the band of grayish-white fur around the animal's neck. Peccaries have heavy, bristly hair that covers a thin, muscular body.

In Arizona, New Mexico, and Texas, collared peccaries are better known as javelinas. The name javelina comes from the Spanish word for javelin or spear. The name refers to the animal's sharp, pointed teeth, which look like small spears. Javelinas have other names as well. They are called baquiro, chacaro, and javali.

Javelinas look much like the wild boars found in Europe. But javelinas are only found in North and South America. There are many physical differences between javelinas and wild boars.

A javelina has just three toes on its hind feet. A wild boar has four toes on each of its feet. Boars have long, sharp tusks that curve upward. Javelinas have short, sharp tusks that grow downward. The tusks are used to dig up roots, seeds, insects, and grub worms.

Javelinas have tough, leathery snouts. As a result, they can eat cactus and other spiny desert plants without hurting their mouths. They also will eat small snakes, lizards, and bugs of all kinds.

The animals live in family groups of five to 15 members. Many families combine to form herds of as many as 50 animals. Herds stay together throughout the year. But each family uses different parts of the herd's territory.

Javelinas have scent glands below each eye and a large one on their backs. The glands produce a strong, skunk-like smell. Javelinas use the smell for identification. Within each family group, javelinas rub faces to mark each other. They rub their backs on rocks and tree trunks to mark herd territory.

The animals have poor vision, fair hearing, but a very good sense of smell. They communicate with grunts, squeals, and short barking noises.

The javelina's enemies include coyotes, bobcats, and mountain lions. When danger is near, the herd will stick together to fight, or scatter quickly in all directions to confuse the enemy. Javelinas are very fast. They can run in bursts of up to 25 miles per hour.

There is just one thing you should always remember. Don't *ever* call them pig!

Tim Trumble

CONRAD J. STORAD grew up in Barberton, Ohio, amidst the belching smokestacks of tire factories, steel mills, and auto assembly plants. He didn't see his first javelina, saguaro cactus, scorpion, or rattlesnake up close and personal until 1982, when he began graduate school at Arizona State University. Currently, Storad is the editor of the nationally award winning *ASU Research Magazine,* and is the founding editor of *Chain Reaction,* a science magazine for young readers. He also is the author of many science and nature books for children and young adults, including the titles: *Don't Ever Cross That Road!, Lizards for Lunch, Little Lords of the Desert, Tarantulas, Scorpions, Sonoran Desert A to Z, and Saguaro Cactus.* Storad lives in Tempe, Arizona with his wife Laurie and their miniature double dapple dachshund, Sophie. They enjoy hiking and exploring the wilds of the Sonoran Desert.

Steve Rolwing

BETH NEELY AND DON RANTZ met in Flagstaff, Arizona at Northern Arizona University. Both studied Fine Art. At NAU, they also discovered a mutual love for the outdoors, gardening, cooking, reading, art, and each other. They married in 1993 and began their artistic collaboration. They now live and work in a small historical bungalow in Prescott, Arizona. They share the house with their two cats, and a backyard menagerie of raccoons, skunks, and coyotes. Members of a small herd of javelinas are frequent visitors. One thing is for certain, Beth and Don will never call them pigs! This is their first children's book.